Molly Lefebure started her writing career as a newspaper reporter in East London during the Blitz. She then worked for many years as the private secretary to the renowned forensic pathologist Dr Keith Simpson, head of the Department of Forensic Medicine at Guy's Hospital. She is the author of several children's books and a memoir of her time working with Dr Simpson, *Murder on the Home Front*, which has been adapted for television. She was a Coleridge scholar and wrote two acclaimed books on the poet, and she was also elected a Fellow of the Royal Society of Literature in 2010. Her two novels for adults, *Blitz* and *Thunder in the Sky*, are sweeping historical sagas and they are closely based on her own experiences during the Second World War. Molly sadly passed away in 2013 but her memory lives on through her writing.

BLITZ

Molly Lefebure

sphere

SPHERE

First published in Great Britain in 1988 by Victor Gollancz Ltd
This paperback edition published in 2014 by Sphere

A CIP catalogue record for this book
is available from the British Library.

ISBN 978-0-7515-5273-7

Typeset in Garamond by M Rules
Printed and bound in Great Britain by
Clays Ltd, St Ives plc

Papers used by Sphere are from well-managed forests
and other responsible sources.

MIX
Paper from
responsible sources
FSC
www.fsc.org
FSC® C104740

Sphere
An imprint of
Little, Brown Book Group
100 Victoria Embankment
London EC4Y 0DY

An Hachette UK Company
www.hachette.co.uk

www.littlebrown.co.uk

For
Margaret de Krassel-Lane

PRINCIPAL CHARACTERS

PAUL DUCHAMP *a surgeon attached to St Jerome's Hospital, London*
ANN DUCHAMP *his wife*
MRS BUSBY *Ann's mother*
ODILE DUCHAMP *elder daughter of Paul and Ann*
MORWENNA DUCHAMP (Thingy) *their second daughter*
ELIZABETH *cook and general domestic in the Duchamp household*
FERNAND LEGRAND *Odile's friend*

SYBIL SPURGEON *next-door neighbour to the Duchamps*
PAM SPURGEON (Jampot) *her daughter*
HUGO SPURGEON *Sybil's elder son*
JASPER SPURGEON *Sybil's younger son*

SIR JOSELIN SOWERSBY *of Parrocks Hall, Stellafield*
LADY SOWERSBY (Dottie) *his wife*
VICKY SOWERSBY *their daughter*
FLIGHT LT. JOSELIN SOWERSBY RAF (Jos) *their elder son*
FRANCIS SOWERSBY (Frank) *their second son*
HARRIET HOPE-WARRINGTON (Hal) *Lady Sowersby's widowed sister*
LAVINIA HOPE-WARRINGTON (Boggy) *her daughter*
NANNY BRADSHAWE *the old family nanny at Parrocks*
ELIOT *butler at Parrocks*
GILES J. SOWERSBY JNR *a distant Sowersby cousin from the US*
HOMER MOUNTJOY *friend of Giles's, also from the US*

FLIGHT LT. PHILIP PLUMBTON RAF (Pongo)
POPPY PLUMBTON *his wife*

MARIE TOOLEY
MICK TOOLEY *her husband*
STEVE TOOLEY *Marie's eldest son*
JOSIE JAMES (née Tooley) *Marie's eldest daughter*
VIOLET POLLOCK *her second daughter*
NELSON TOOLEY *Marie's second son*
RHONA TOOLEY *her third daughter*
PETE TOOLEY *Marie's youngest, and last, child*
GERT POLLOCK *Marie's sister*

POSY COWPER *full-time District Air Raid Warden, ARP*
FLO COWPER *her widowed mother*
HENRY COWPER *Flo Cowper's only son, Posy's brother*
MRS LOFTUS *housekeeper to Ernie Cowper, Flo's brother-in-law*

THE REVEREND CLEM IRVING *a young curate with an East End Mission*
SISTER SUNFLOWER-LUPIN *sister of Sunflower-Lupin Ward at Plashett Wold Burns Unit*
Miss ISABELLA WIDGEON *warden of Tulip House*
MISS HONORA WHITEBEAM *her assistant, friend and lifelong companion*
LILY *servant at Tulip House*

Part One

CRY HAVOC

I

Posy Cowper, a full-time salaried District Air Raid Warden attached to Cuddwell Number Seven Post, stood at the junction of Unity Street and Tollemache Terrace scowling and casting impatient glances at her watch. The time was precisely ten minutes past ten. The air raid had been in progress for ten minutes. Three minutes after the warning had sounded a bomb had dropped on the Post Office in front of which Posy was now standing. The Post Office had been reduced to a pile of rubble; it had been fairly busy at the time of the incident and several people who, at the sound of the warning, had raced out of the building in an attempt to reach the basement air raid shelter at the further end of Tollemache Terrace had been caught by bomb blast and flying glass. An ambulance had arrived upon the scene with admirable promptitude and had removed six walking wounded. Four other persons, all seriously injured, remained lying upon the pavement awaiting help.

An ARP Heavy Rescue lorry now drove up and five members of personnel tumbled out. Their leader, in ordinary life known to Posy as her local newsagent, advanced and said, 'Morning, Pose. Any idea how many people may be trapped under the ruins? Heard any cries for help?'

'Not a sound,' responded Posy tersely.

The squad vanished to the rear of the Post Office. Posy remained in position on the street corner. The casualties lay motionless and silent where they had fallen. Otherwise Posy had the place to herself. From a distance came sounds of shouting, whistles blowing, ambulance and fire-brigade bells shrilling and clanging. Posy, who loved to be in the thick of things, shifted her feet and muttered impatiently. On her head was her steel helmet, her respirator in its canvas bag was slung at the 'Ready' position on her chest. Completely prepared and on the alert, looking capable of coping single-handed with any number of Germans should they suddenly come round the corner, Posy glared hard at nothing.

'Excuse me, Miss Cowper, might I have a word with you please?'

The voice came from a small wispy girl in a belted raincoat who had suddenly appeared from nowhere and stood holding a notebook and pencil at the ready as she stared up at Posy with big, earnest, blue eyes. Posy rasped, 'What d'you want, Miss Duchamp?'

'If you could tell me a few details about this incident. The *Gazette* wants a big story on this . . .'

Posy cut the girl short. 'Your editor should know better than to send his reporters to take up the time of people like me in an air raid. All I'm telling you is that you, as a civilian, when an air raid alert sounds, should take the nearest available cover and remain there till you hear the all-clear.'

'But Miss Cowper, as a reporter it's my job to find out what's going on and to . . .'

'I don't care what your job is, you're a civilian and it's your duty to get under cover and keep out of danger. We've already got enough casualties to deal with without adding you to the list. So off you go, see?' Little Morwenna Duchamp, obviously realizing that further argument was pointless, folded her notebook and scuttled away up the street. Posy, with an expression of satisfaction, watched her retreating figure. Miss Duchamp, who had only recently come to

work on the *Cuddwell Gazette*, had found digs in Posy's m
house, and, though a pleasant enough little girl, should not
attempted to take advantage of a privileged position; at least, that
was how Posy saw it. Miss Duchamp wouldn't dare to ask any other
member of ARP personnel for help with her newspaper story! All
members of Civil Defence knew that they mustn't give the press
details of enemy attacks, or anyone else come to that. It was a simple
matter of national security. There was an official Information Officer
and the *Cuddwell Gazette* should have approached him. Little
Morwenna Duchamp needed to learn to mind her Ps and Qs.

After which, Posy Cowper once more glared at her watch.
Where on earth were those ambulances for the other casualties?
She herself had been on the scene of the incident within minutes
of the bomb falling and had summoned assistance without delay.
Since when, apart from removal of the walking wounded (who
hadn't required transport) and the arrival of Heavy Rescue (who
had now disappeared) absolutely nothing had happened. What a
way to fight a war!

At length, unable to stand this inactivity any longer, Posy strode
rapidly up Unity Street, blowing angry blasts on her whistle as she
went. These blasts should have brought fellow ARP workers has-
tening to her; but not a soul appeared.

She turned out of Unity Street and almost at once tripped over
an enormous hose-pipe. This, like a giant anaconda, squirmed
along the gutter in the direction of a throng of firemen and ambulance men jostling among a viscera of hose-pipes outside
Woolworths, watched by a crowd of sightseers, including Morwenna Duchamp. Posy bore down upon this assembly. She
plunged among the sightseers, 'Hey you, take cover! This is an air
raid, not a Punch and Judy show!'

A couple of St John's Ambulance men were in the crowd; Posy
leapt upon them like a tigress. 'I'm looking for some of you lot!

There's four bad casualties lying outside the Post Office, dying for want of help!'

'Keep your hair on, duck. We know all about them; all under control. Ambulance on its way there now.'

'Under control my foot! I summoned an ambulance twenty minutes ago!'

'Out of the way, out of the way there please!' A fireman, all brass, leather and authority, pushed Posy back into the crowd; at the same time a Salvation Army officer, carrying a bawling toddler who had lost his mother, collided heavily with her, almost knocking her off her feet. 'Out of the way please!'

Posy declared, loudly, to nobody in particular, 'I wash my hands of this bedlam!' She returned to the Post Office. No wonder, she thought to herself, they were calling this a Phoney War!

It was April 1940. Posy had been one of London's air raid wardens for the past two years; she was also an instructor in first aid, holding classes not only in her home borough of Cuddwell, but in a number of other eastern suburbs into the bargain. She was recognized as a first-rate instructor; wasn't ashamed of admitting it herself.

The recruits who attended her classes saw before them a strapping, strident-voiced spinster in her mid-thirties; firm-jowled, her hair cut in a no-nonsense shingle, the glance of her sharp eyes dauntingly direct, her eyebrows heavy and well marked. There was universal astonishment when it leaked out that this brawny, boot-faced Amazon rejoiced in the name of 'Posy'.

Posy prided herself upon being a pragmatist. As early as 1936 she had decided that it was well on the cards that the rise of Hitler's Germany would result in another war and therefore she had started attending first-aid classes and lectures on fire-fighting and anti-gas precautions; in spite of the fact that at this point in